For Janice Thomson —
Thanks for everything, Wise Owl.
J.W. and T.R.

STERLING and the distinctive Sterling logo are registered trademarks of Sterling Publishing Co., Inc.

Library of Congress Cataloging-in-Publication Data Available

2 4 6 8 10 9 7 5 3 1

Published in 2008 by Sterling Publishing Co., Inc.
387 Park Avenue South, New York, NY 10016

First published in Great Britain in 2006 by Andersen Press Ltd.
20 Vauxhall Bridge Road, London SW1V 2SA, UK

© 2006 text by Jeanne Willis
© 2006 illustrations by Tony Ross

First published in the United States in 2008 by Sterling Publishing Co., Inc.
387 Park Avenue South, New York, NY 10016
Distributed in Canada by Sterling Publishing
c/o Canadian Manda Group, 165 Dufferin Street
Toronto, Ontario, Canada M6K 3H6

Printed in Singapore

Sterling ISBN 978-1-4027-6346-5

For information about custom editions, special sales, premium and corporate purchases,
please contact Sterling Special Sales Department at 800-805-5489 or specialsales@sterlingpublishing.com.

DAFT BAT

Jeanne Willis and Tony Ross

STERLING

New York / London

There was once a bat who got everything the wrong way around.

At least that's what the wild young animals thought.

It all started when Bat first arrived.

Owl wanted to give her a welcome gift,
so he asked the wild young animals
to go and find out what she would like.

"I'd like an umbrella to keep my feet dry, please," she said.

"Umbrellas keep *heads* dry, not feet!" whispered Baby Elephant. "Daft Bat!"

"Anyone can make a mistake," said Goat Kid.

So they thought no more about it and gave her a fancy new umbrella.

But then Bat said another very odd thing.

She said, "I'm so glad you brought me an umbrella. There's a big, black rain cloud in the sky below."

"Daft Bat!" giggled Giraffe Calf.
"The sky is *above*, not below!"

And then Bat said another funny thing.

"If it rains very hard the river will rise and my ears will get wet," she said.

"But if the river rises our *toes* will get wet, not our ears!" growled Lion Cub.

"I would wear a rain hat, but it would only fall off into the grass above," Bat added.

"But the grass isn't above, it's *below!*" muttered Rhino Junior. "What a daft bat she is!"

By now, all the wild young animals
thought Bat was completely crazy.

So they ran off to tell Owl.

"Bat's bonkers! She's berserk!" said Baby Elephant.
"If she's crazy, she might be dangerous!" said Lion Cub.
"Help!" said Goat Kid.

"Why do you think Bat is crazy?" hooted Owl.

"She sees things differently than we do," said Rhino Junior.
"Very differently," said Giraffe Calf.

Owl looked thoughtful. Then he said, "I will ask Bat some simple questions and I will decide who is crazy."

So they all went to visit Bat. Owl asked if she would mind answering a few questions. "Not at all," she said.

"Question Number One," said Owl.
"What does a tree look like?"

"That's easy," said Bat. "A tree has a trunk
at the top and leaves at the bottom."

"See, Owl? Bat is daft!" laughed Giraffe Calf.
"A tree has a trunk at the *bottom* and leaves
at the *top*. Even I know that!"

"Question Number Two!" said Owl.
"What does a mountain look like?"

"That's even easier!" said Bat. "A mountain has a flat bit at the top and a pointy bit hanging down."

"You daft bat! The pointy bit of a mountain sticks *up*, not down!" said Goat Kid. "I know, I'm a mountain goat." "Bat is looney!" they all cried. "Call the doctor!"

"Last question!" said Owl. "And I'd like everyone to answer it, except Bat."
"All right," said the wild young animals.
"What's the question?"

And Owl said, "Question Number Three! Have you ever tried looking at things from *Bat's* point of view?"

And he made them all hang upside down
from a branch — just like Bat.

"Oooh," said Goat Kid. "Bat was right! When you look at it
this way, the pointy bit of the mountain does hang down!"
"And the tree has a trunk at the *top* and leaves at the
bottom," said Giraffe Calf.

"Heeey! The grass is *above* our heads!"
said Rhino Junior. "And the sky . . . isn't!"

Just then it started to rain.
It rained and rained and rained.

"Can I get down now, Owl? The river is rising.
  My ears are wet!" said Lion Cub.
"And my feet are getting soaked from this angle!"
said Baby Elephant.

So Bat lent him her fancy new umbrella to keep them all dry.

"Thank you," he said. "I'm so sorry I said you were looney."
"We're all sorry," said the wild young animals.

"Oh . . . don't be daft!" smiled Bat.